Lights, Camera, Middle School!

A Yearling Book

JENNIFER L. HOLM & MATTHEW HOLM

BABYMOUSE
TALES FROM THE LOCKER

Lights, Camera, Middle School!

This is a work of fiction. Names, characters, places, and incidents either are the product of the authors' imagination or are used fictitiously. Any resemblance to actual persons, living or dead, events, or locales is entirely coincidental.

Copyright © 2017 by Jennifer Holm and Matthew Holm

All rights reserved. Published in the United States by Yearling, an imprint of Random House Children's Books, a division of Penguin Random House LLC, New York. Originally published in hardcover in the United States by Random House Children's Books, a division of Penguin Random House LLC, New York, in 2017.

Yearling and the jumping horse design are registered trademarks of Penguin Random House LLC.

Visit us on the Web! rhcbooks.com

Educators and librarians, for a variety of teaching tools, visit us at RHTeachersLibrarians.com

The Library of Congress has cataloged the hardcover edition of this work as follows:
Names: Holm, Jennifer L., author. | Holm, Matthew.
Title: Lights, camera, middle school! / by Jennifer L. Holm & Matthew Holm.
Description: First edition. | New York : Random House, [2017] |
Series: Babymouse. Tales from the Locker | Summary: "Babymouse joins the school Film Club and writes the greatest cinematic masterpiece of all time! But when the movie gets shown to the entire school, will it be a box office hit or a flop?" —Provided by publisher.
Identifiers: LCCN 2016014341 | ISBN 978-0-399-55438-4 (hardcover) | ISBN 978-0-399-55440-7 (ebook)
Subjects: LCSH: Graphic novels. | CYAC: Graphic novels. | Motion pictures—Production and direction—Fiction. | Middle schools—Fiction. | Schools—Fiction. | Mice—Fiction. | Animals—Fiction. | Humorous stories.
Classification: LCC PZ7.7.H65 Li 2017 | DDC 741.5/973—dc23

ISBN 978-0-593-42829-0 (paperback)

Printed in the United States of America
10 9 8 7 6 5 4 3 2 1
First Yearling Edition 2022

For Caden

—J.L.H.

For Kevin, who always put me in his movies

—M.H.

Contents

Monster Movie

Middle school was like a movie.

Not a romantic-smoochy movie or a swashbuckling-pirate movie. Or even a space-aliens-invade-the-world kind of movie.

It was a **monster movie**.

The hallways were crawling with spooky creatures.

You were always having to run for your life.

And everywhere you turned, someone was trying to eat your brains.

But sometimes the scariest thing about middle school involved **whiskers.**

And, believe me, I know whiskers.

My name is Babymouse.

And this is my Tale from the Locker.

I was standing in front of my locker, trying to open it. As usual, the door was stuck. I had a love-hate relationship with my locker, aka "Locker." Mostly I hated the big metal bully. (I swear it ate my homework!)

I banged on it for a minute, and finally it popped open.

"Hey, Babymouse," a voice called.

I turned around to see Felicia Furrypaws.

If this was a monster movie, Felicia would be a Zombie. At middle school, Zombies travelled in packs and dressed the same. Instead of hunting brains, they wanted **stuff**: whatever was cool and "in." It could be wedge sandals or ruffled scarves or sparkly lip gloss. They just **had** to have it.

Felicia and I had gone to elementary school together. With her perfectly straight whiskers, she had always been one of the popular girls. Today, she was sporting a plaid skirt, white tights, and a crisp white shirt with a ruffled bow. She looked stylish and French, like she'd walked out of a fashion ad. Her look shouted "Cool Girl."

And my look? I wasn't quite sure. I definitely wanted my look to say:

I'M SWEET!

I'M SENSITIVE!

I'M CLEVER!

FMP!

ZAP!

I'M DARING!

But I also wanted my look to say a lot of other things, including:

I LOVE BOOKS!

I THINK KOALA BEARS ARE UNDERAPPRECIATED!

I KNOW A LOT OF KNOCK-KNOCK JOKES!

KNOCK KNOCK!

NO MORE!

I'M A GOOD CONVERSATIONALIST!

I KNOW THREE FRENCH WORDS!

C'EST LA VIE.

It was kind of hard to translate all this into a "look."

Speaking of looks, Felicia was staring at my face.

"Did you straighten your whiskers?" she asked.

"Yes!" I said with a bright smile.

It was technically true. My whiskers were straight, even if they weren't exactly mine. See, I'd tried straightening my whiskers using a fancy cream, but the harsh chemicals had burned them right off. So this morning, I'd glued on some false whiskers to hide the damage.

"You might want to use more glue next time," she told me.

"What do you mean?" I asked.

"That," she said, pointing at my nose. I realized that one of my whiskers was ... dangling?

She blew at it.

I watched in horror as it fell off and floated to the floor in slow motion.

Felicia walked off, laughing.

Le sigh.

I was never going to be famous for my whiskers.

And **that** was the problem right there.

In elementary school, all I wanted to do was fit in. But now that I was in middle school, I wanted to stand out.

I wanted to be the one **everyone** was talking about!

I wanted to be Famous.

Mostly because I wanted a private jet. (The school bus was seriously stinky.)

The warning bell for first period rang. I couldn't be late again. Mr. Ludwig was a lizard, and in addition to being cold-blooded, he was a stickler for being on time to homeroom. Which made no sense to me at all. You didn't actually learn anything in homeroom. You just had to sit there and listen to announcements.

I searched through the bottom of my locker for my algebra book, but it wasn't there. I turned to the boy who had the locker next to mine.

"Georgie," I asked, "could you look on the top shelf of my locker and see if my algebra book is there?"

Georgie was like a movie star. Except instead of tall, dark, and handsome, he was tall, yellow, and ... spotted.

"Sure, Babymouse," he said. He reached up easily and pulled out my book.

"Thanks," I said. "What are you going to sign up for?"

It was Activities Week. This was when kids signed up for extracurricular clubs and sports. And there were so many choices!

Georgie shrugged. "I'm not sure yet. Definitely not basketball."

He was a little sensitive about his height. He'd been asked to join the basketball team every year since he was in kindergarten.

"See you later," Georgie said with a little wave, trudging down the hall and pulling his roller bag.

The bell rang again, and I started to push my locker door shut. But it wouldn't click closed. What if there was a real monster in my locker? I'll admit that sometimes my imagination could run away with me. . . .

HEEEEEYYYYY!!!

Riiiiiiiiiiiiiing!

The ringing bell woke me from my daydream, and I found myself standing in an empty school hallway.

And I realized I was late for homeroom. Again.

Typical.

Laws of the Jungle Cafeteria

The hardest subject in middle school wasn't science or social studies or literature.

It was friendship.

And there was no textbook or helpful study guide. In elementary school, if kids didn't like you, they were just flat-out mean. But here, figuring out who your friends were was harder than a quadratic equation.

And I had a failing grade.

GOOD FRIENDS (AKA "THE GANG") ☆

1. ~~Felicia~~
2. Wilson
3. Georgie
4. Penny
5. Duckie
6. ~~Henry~~

KINDA SOMETIMES FRIENDS

1. Felicia
2. Henry ???
3. ~~Melinda~~
4. ~~Belinda~~
5. ~~Berry~~

PRETTY SURE NOT FRIENDS AND MAY EVEN HATE ME

1. Melinda (Meanie)
2. Belinda (Miney)
3. Berry (Mo)
4. Locker

NO CLUE AT ALL

1. Everybody else in the school

Speaking of equations, my first-period class was math. Talk about starting the day on a bad whisker.

Blergh.

We were doing algebra, and I wasn't a fan. In fact, I hated it. (Then again, does algebra have any fans?)

The math teacher, Ms. Calculate (her name really was Ms. Calculate!!!!!!), moved way too fast. Not that this was a surprise— she was an octopus.

Today, she was reviewing variables and coefficients.

"A coefficient is a number that multiplies a variable," she told the class.

The only thing that was being multiplied around here was boringness.

$$\text{Algebra} \times \text{Middle School} = (\text{Boringness})^{100}$$

I wished I was anywhere but here. Besides, if I was Famous, I wouldn't have to go to math class.

CREAK!

GLAMOUR!

THERE SHE IS!

"Babymouse!"

I blinked my eyes open to see Ms. Calculate pointing at me with all eight legs.

(Talk about crash-landing back to Earth.)

"Babymouse. What is the coefficient in the problem on the board?"

I stared at the problem. Maybe I should start paying attention?

"Uh, the coefficient is **xyz** over 0?" I suggested.

She shook her head.

"Or **abc** over 123?" I said, trying again.

Her lips thinned.

I gave up. "One plus two equals three?"

Luckily, the bell rang at that moment, and I was free! But as I stepped through the door, I heard Ms. Calculate's voice.

"Babymouse, please come see me after school so we can discuss your ability to pay attention."

Stupid algebra.

☆ ♡ ☆

I may have hated math, but I loathed lunch.

Yes, **loathed.**

All those cranky, hungry kids roaming free made the cafeteria seem like a jungle. And just like in the jungle, there were Laws.

LAWS OF THE CAFETERIA

1. The hot lunch is usually cold.

2. Avoid the chicken patties at all costs.

3. Condiments, condiments, condiments!

4. Do not trip or spill anything, or everyone will give you a weird look.

5. Always have a plan for where to sit.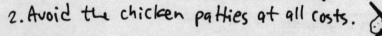

6. Always have a backup plan for where to sit.

7. And a backup backup plan.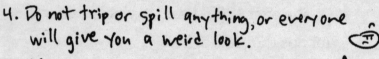

8. If you can't find anyone to sit with, pretend you don't care. SHRUG

9. Eat fast.

10. Get out of the cafeteria as soon as possible. The library is a good refuge.

Today, the ~~hot~~ lukewarm lunch was teriyaki chicken with baby peas. The teriyaki chicken looked like mush, and the peas were gray.

After I made it through the lunch line, I looked for a place to sit. I spotted an open seat next to Felicia and walked over.

"Is this seat taken?" I asked her.

Her minion Melinda waved her hands. "Totally taken."

Belinda said, "Taken since ten minutes ago."

Berry added, "Taken since the fall of Rome."

But it was pretty obvious to me that no one was sitting there.

"Sorry, Babymouse," Felicia said. "Maybe some other time."

As I walked away, I thought I heard them laughing.

I circled the cafeteria, looking for a

friendly face. I was about to give up and sit with a smelly boy when I heard someone call my name. (Nothing personal about the smelly boy—he was a skunk.)

"Babymouse!"

I looked across the room and saw my best friend, Wilson, waving at me.

"Over here, Babymouse!" Wilson called.

We'd been BFFs forever. In my opinion, everyone needed a weaselly best friend.

"I saved you a seat," Wilson told me.

"Thanks," I said.

Penny and Duckie were sitting there, too.

"Hi, Penny! Do you know what club you're going to join?"

"I'd like to sign up for Cheer, but it's pretty competitive," she said.

As a poodle, she was naturally peppy. I could totally see her as a cheerleader.

"Maybe I'll try out for Cheer, too," I said.

She looked at me. "How are your back handsprings?"

"Back handsprings? I thought you just had to wave pom-poms and shout."

Penny shook her head. "It's a serious sport, Babymouse."

That sounded **too hard.**

"What do you think about Handball Club,

Babymouse?" Wilson suggested.

"What do you do?"

"You just hit a ball against the wall," he said.

That sounded **too easy.**

"I know!" Duckie said. "You should sign up for Recycling Club."

"Don't tell me. You recycle trash?"

"Exactly!" he exclaimed.

That sounded **too boring.**

Goldilocks had it way easy. All she had to do was find the right bed!

The bell signaling the end of lunch rang, and everyone started to pack up. When I walked out of the cafeteria, there was a crowd huddled around the Activities Sign-Up Board. I pushed my way to the front.

And then I saw it.

Film Club?

I smiled slowly. This was my chance to be Famous.

This was **just right.**

Epic Fail?

I wanted to be prepared for Film Club, so I started doing what seemed obvious: watching movies.

My mom said I should watch comedies. My dad said I should watch romances. My little brother, Squeak, said I should watch cartoons. And my grandfather? He said I should watch movies about clowns. (Uh, yeah, Grampamouse could be a bit wacky.)

In the end, I watched . . . **everything.**

I discovered that I loved the sweeping period epics. I loved everything about them. The way they took place in exotic countries. How the costumes were so elaborate.

And, of course, the elephants.

I'm not sure why there were always elephants in epics, but I kind of liked it.

That was when I knew: I wanted to make movies like **this**. Movies that swept you away to a different time and place. Where everything was exciting and—

"This is boring, Babymouse," Squeak said.

—and there were no annoying Littles.

Squeak was a Little, aka little brother.

I pointed at the television. "What are you talking about? This is an amazing movie!"

He yawned.

"They shot it in Paris and Japan and India! What about those costumes? Did you see all those petticoats? **Did you see those elephants?**"

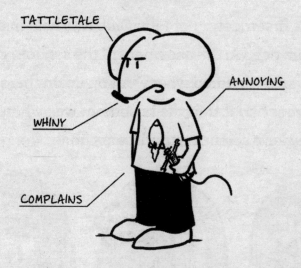

TATTLETALE

ANNOYING

WHINY

COMPLAINS

"Boring," he repeated. "I want to watch **Squish.**"

What did he know anyway? His favorite show was an animated series about an amoeba. Seriously, an amoeba?

"Can I have the remote?" he asked. "You've had it for the last two days. And you're getting kind of smelly."

"Fine," I said, and slapped the remote control into his hand. "Enjoy your single-celled organism."

The first meeting of Film Club was held in a room deep in the basement of the school. I'd always wondered what went on down there. Rumor had it that the basement was where they kept science experiments gone wrong.

Walking down the dark staircase and into the basement was like something out of a horror movie. The mildewy hallway. The lights flicking off and on. The water drip-drip-dripping...

Drip. Drip. Drip.

DRIP

DRIP

CREEEAAAAK!

WHIP!

WHAT'S THAT?

CLAP!

AAAGGHH!

WHIP!

HEY, BABYMOUSE.

Wilson, Penny, Georgie, and Duckie were standing there.

"You all joined Film Club?" I asked Wilson.

"It was either this or Clowning Club," he said with a shrug.

"Clowns scare me," Penny admitted.

I was pretty sure they scared everybody except my grandfather.

I looked around the room. Movie posters papered the walls. In one corner was a pile of lighting equipment. Next to it was a metal suitcase that said "Audio." There were coils of orange extension cords and a milk crate full of black tape. A bat and a bear stood off to the side, apparently wanting to join the club, too.

"Hello, future filmmakers!" a voice called.

We all turned to see a teacher enter the room.

"My name is Ms. Octavia, and I'm the Film Club adviser. I used to work in Hollywood, and I'm looking forward to sharing my experience with you."

"What did you do?" I asked her.

"I was a screenwriter."

"Wow! That must have been exciting!" I said.

She gave me a look. "I suppose you'll find out. Because the whole purpose of Film Club is to actually **make** a film. From conception to screen."

Then she started to tick off her fingers. "You will write the script. Cast the film. Secure locations. Make props. Design scenery. Sew costumes. Set up lights. Film. Record audio. Edit. When the film is complete, you will screen it for the entire middle school," she finished.

There was silence as everyone looked around the room.

"It's important to remember that film-making is a **collaborative** experience. Let's get started. The first thing you need to do as a group is to figure out what genre of film you would like to produce."

Wilson's hand shot up. "Monster movie all the way!"

"Romance!" Penny said. "Something dreamy!"

"What about a detective movie? Classic noir," Duckie suggested.

Georgie bent his head down. "I have a movie idea."

"What is it?" I asked him.

"It's about a boy who is struggling to find his place in the world. He meets a furry monster named Bigfoot, and they bond and become each other's best friends. They set out on a road trip across the country. Along the way, they discover a hidden realm of troublesome gnomes. The gnomes decide to join them. As they near a desert, a spaceship crashes and aliens emerge. The aliens need help getting home, so the boy and Bigfoot and the troublesome gnomes help to rebuild the aliens' spaceship. Then the aliens take them all to space. The end."

Everyone stared up at Georgie in shock. It was always the tall, quiet ones with the roller bags who had the best imaginations.

"What?" he said, blushing. "It's just something I've been tossing around."

I piped up. "So . . . kind of like an epic? I think we should make an epic!"

"An epic?" the bat-girl asked. Her name was Lucy.

"An epic has all these elements. Romance. Drama. Mystery."

Everyone nodded.

"Well done, Babymouse," Ms. Octavia praised me. "Since you were successful in bringing everyone to a consensus, it only makes sense for you to be the director."

I gasped. "Me?"

Ms. Octavia smiled. "Yes, Babymouse. You."

I. Was. The. Director.

"And since it's your vision you'll be bringing to the screen, you're also going to be responsible for writing the screenplay," Ms. Octavia added.

"You mean I have to **write** it?" That sounded like **work**.

She nodded. "That's exactly what I'm saying, Babymouse."

Le sigh.

A Dark and Squeaky Night

I stared at the computer screen.

OPEN ON A DARK NIGHT.

Right after school, I had locked myself in my bedroom and gotten down to work. Now, hours later, I only had one line. Who knew that making things up could be so **hard**?

Hmmm . . . Maybe I just needed to channel my inner writer. Into feelings and desires. Like for a softer chair. And maybe a good book and . . .

No! I needed to focus! I needed to think BIG. Bigger than BIG. Epic-BIG!

How did you say "big" in French, anyway?

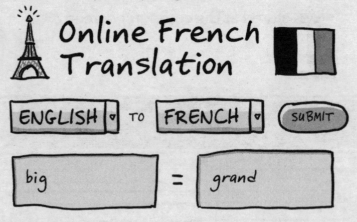

That was it! The Eiffel Tower was indeed **grand.**

EXT. PARIS—NIGHT

We see the Eiffel Tower in the distance.

Whew! That was a good start. Perfect setting. Where would I go from there?

My stomach rumbled. When was dinner anyway?

EXT. SIDEWALK CAFÉ—NIGHT

VERONIQUE is sitting at a table. We see the Eiffel Tower in the distance.

A waiter delivers a TASTY CUPCAKE to her.

My door banged open, and my annoying Little was standing there.

"Babymouse!" Squeak said. "I can't find the charger for my WHIZ BANG™. Have you seen it?"

"I'm busy being brilliant, Squeak."

"But, Babymouse—"

I cut him off. **"Au revoir!"**

"What does that mean?"

"It's French for 'Good-bye!'" I said, look-ing at him. "And close the door on your way out. I'm creating a masterpiece here!"

He rolled his eyes and left, slamming the door.

I looked back at my screen.


```
EXT. SIDEWALK CAFÉ—NIGHT


VERONIQUE is sitting at a table. We
see the Eiffel Tower in the distance.


A waiter delivers a TASTY CUPCAKE to her.


        VERONIQUE

    Merci.
```

```
A MYSTERIOUS FIGURE walks up. He's
tall and wears a hat.

          MYSTERIOUS FIGURE
     Excuse me, mademoiselle. I seem to
     have lost something.
```

The door to my room banged open again.

"Can I borrow **your** charger, Baby-mouse?" Squeak asked, holding up his WHIZ BANG™.

I shook my head. **"Non!"**

(That was French for "No!" I was on a roll.)

He made a face and slammed back out.

Honestly, how was I expected to create in an environment like this? It wasn't at all suitable for being artistic. Maybe I just needed something to get me in the mood? I looked around, and my eyes landed on my own WHIZ BANG™. I put in my earbuds and cranked up some classical music.

There. Perfect.

EXT. SIDEWALK CAFÉ—NIGHT

VERONIQUE is sitting at a table. We
see the Eiffel Tower in the distance.

A waiter delivers a TASTY CUPCAKE to
her.

    VERONIQUE
  <u>Merci.</u>

A MYSTERIOUS FIGURE walks up. He's
tall and wears a hat.

    MYSTERIOUS FIGURE
  Excuse me, <u>mademoiselle.</u> I seem to
  have lost something. Have you seen
  my . . .

VERONIQUE looks up from her cupcake.

        VERONIQUE
    Yes?

        MYSTERIOUS FIGURE
    WHIZ BANG™ charger?

No! No!

NON!

AAAGGGHHHHHH!

This was all wrong!

NO WHIZ BANGS™!!!

I put my face in my hands and thought hard. This scene needed **something**. I closed my eyes and tried to imagine it.

But what? It needed something exciting. Something dramatic. Something exotic. Something epic. It needed . . .

ELEPHANTS.

My door slammed open.

"Babymouse!"

I glared at my annoying Little. "What?"

He shrugged.

"Mom said to come downstairs. Dinner's ready."

Le grand sigh.

Director's Chair

The next day after school, I bounced into Film Club with copies of my screenplay. Excitement hummed through my whiskers as I passed them out.

Georgie looked up from the script. "**Au Revoir, My Locker**?"

"Yes," I said. "**Au revoir** means 'good-bye' in French. It's an existential epic where the heroine reconsiders her place in the world."

"Are there monsters?" Wilson asked.

"Yep!" I told him.

"Romance?" Penny asked.

"Check!"

"Did you include Bigfoot?" Georgie asked wistfully.

"And troublesome gnomes," I told him with a grin.

He smiled. "Thanks, Babymouse."

"It certainly sounds **interesting**, Baby-mouse," Ms. Octavia said.

I beamed.

"Well, now that you have a script, you can start pre-production. This is the part of the filmmaking process where you organize for the actual shoot. Your crew needs to be assigned to specific departments."

We passed the list around the room, and people signed up for various jobs.

No one wanted to be an assistant. (Not that I blamed them.)

CREW

Director: _Babymouse ♡_

Producer: _Duckie_

Camera~~man~~ bat: _Lucy_

Sound Recorder: _Caden_

Scenery/Props: _Wilson_

Wardrobe & Makeup & Hair: _Penny_

Lights: _Georgie_

Assistants: _____

The crew decided to start meeting at lunch to give us more time to plan.

Most of the crew I already knew. But I hadn't hung out with Lucy much in elementary school, although I knew her. She was totally channeling a whole new style for middle school—the Goth look.

Caden was a complete mystery. He was either shy or just quiet, because he didn't say a word. Maybe it was a bear thing.

"Hey, gang," I said as I sat down. "Did you read my script?"

They all looked at me.

"It's pretty good, Babymouse," Wilson said.

I puffed up with pride.

"Thanks!" I said. "And you know what? I already have the sequel all figured out!"

"The sequel?" Georgie asked.

"Of course!" I said. "This is just the **first** movie. All the famous directors have sequels lined up."

Duckie looked concerned. "Before we start talking about the next movie, we should probably talk about **this** one, right?"

"Okay," I agreed. "Hit me."

Penny pulled out a notebook of sketches. "For wardrobe, I'm thinking we do lots of period costumes." She pointed to the sketches. "Skirts, little details."

"Those look great," I told her.

"What do you think about shooting some of the scenes in black and white?" Lucy asked me. "Might give it a real film noir look."

"That sounds great!"

We were on a roll! And then Duckie frowned.

"I'm a little concerned about locations," he said.

"Why?"

Duckie flipped open his notebook. "You

have twenty locations in the screenplay. And some of them are pretty exotic." He started to rattle them off. "A spooky forest in Belgium. A café in Paris. A castle in England—"

"It **is** an epic."

"An epic with no budget," he clarified.

My heart sank. "So that means no Paris?"

He shook his head.

"What about the castle?"

"Yeah, uh, no."

My whiskers twitched, just as they always did when I got anxious. "What are we going to do?"

Lucy squeaked, "I have an idea! We can cheat it."

"What do you mean?" I asked her.

"You don't actually have to be in Paris for people to think you're there. Make the shot tight!"

Wilson nodded. "Right! And dress the set with French props so it feels like Paris."

I felt better already.

Then I remembered.

"Can we still have elephants?" I asked.

Duckie rolled his eyes and shrugged. "I'll see what I can do."

☆ ♥ ☆

Now that my crew was in place, I needed to cast the actors.

I taped flyers around the school, advertising the casting call. I figured I'd be flooded with people wanting to audition. Everybody wanted to be a movie star.

And I mean **everybody**.

When I walked into the cafeteria for lunch, I heard someone calling my name.

"Yoo-hoo! Babymouse!"

I looked around and could hardly believe what I saw:

We saved you a seat! Felicia mouthed to me as she pointed to the empty seat next to her.

I felt like I was in an alternate reality. One where I was **cool.**

"This is the best seat," Meanie said.

"The very best," Miney said.

"Like Queen of the Universe Best," Mo added.

I couldn't deny that I had always thought this was a better table—and it really was. The chairs were padded. There were fresh flowers. And they had amazing condiments: spicy sriracha mayo and soy sauce and pink salt!

I was in heaven.

Felicia shared her sushi with me as we discussed everything under the sun. Did whisker straighteners really work? (Sometimes.) Should you ever wear nude panty hose? (Never.) Were black patent Mary Jane shoes fashionable? (Always.)

At the end of lunch when the bell rang, Felicia smiled at me. "See you at auditions!"

That was when I realized what was going on: Felicia wasn't interested in **me**.

She was interested in getting a part.

Typical.

☆ ♥ ☆

Unfortunately, it turned out Drama Club was holding its auditions at the same time as us.

Stupid musical theater. They had such an unfair advantage with their catchy tunes.

Felicia was the first person to audition for the film.

"What role are you interested in?" I asked her.

"Veronique, of course," she said, flashing her straight whiskers.

"Do you speak French? I want Veronique to have an authentic accent," I told her.

"But of course," Felicia replied.

"Can you say something in French?"

"Oui," she said.

Le sigh.

"Do you have any film experience?"

"Haven't you seen my video on the Internet? It has two thousand likes."

Of course.

"Let's get started. Duckie will read the lines for the Mysterious Figure. Ready? And . . . action!"

DO YOU NEED HELP.

PLEASE HELP ME, SIR!

I SEEM TO BE LOST!

WINCE

CAN YOU PULL IT BACK A LITTLE?

I GUESS SO.

DO YOU NEED HE

PLEEAASSE HEELLLLP ME, SIR!

I SEEM TO BE LOOSSSTTT!

IF THAT WAS HER PULLING IT BACK, I'D HATE TO SEE HER BEING MORE DRAMATIC.

ERP.

THANK YOU, FELICIA.

NEXT!

?

SEND IN THE NEXT ACTOR TRYING OUT FOR VERONIQUE.

ANYBODY? ANYBODY?

CAN I TRY OUT, BABYMOUSE? I AM A CLASSICALLY TRAINED NARRATOR.

LE SIGH.

SLUMP

Action!

I had my cast!

AU REVOIR, MY LOCKER CAST LIST

VERONIQUE: *Felicia*

MYSTERIOUS FIGURE: *Henry*

BIGFOOT: *Georgie*

WAITER: *Georgie*

NEWSBOY: *Georgie*

CARRIAGE DRIVER: *Georgie*

SCULLERY MAID: *Georgie*

GIRAFFE IN ZOO: *Georgie*

When the first day of shooting arrived, we all gathered after school. I was so excited that I could barely keep my whiskers straight. And they had been pretty straight lately. (It turned out that Felicia knew a thing or two about whiskers. I'd been using a mousse she'd suggested.)

The first scene was supposed to take place in a spooky forest. Duckie had scouted around the school and found what he said was a perfect spot.

"What do you think?" he asked.

"Uh, Duckie," I said to him. "This doesn't look very, um, **spooky**."

"Use your imagination," he said.

"WITH IMAGINATION"

"It's not working for me," I told him.

"Sorry. It's what's in the budget."

I gave him a questioning look.

"Free," he explained.

"We have to do something!" I told him.

Duckie looked at the location. "Maybe we can make it work if we dress it?"

"You want to put a dress on a bush?" I asked.

"'To dress a set' means to add props, Babymouse. Let's see if Wilson has any ideas."

Wilson came over and checked out the location.

"It's supposed to be a spooky forest," I explained.

Wilson scratched his head. "I have some fake cobwebs I can put on the bushes and a few plastic spiders. That might make it a little spookier. But I don't have a whole forest."

"It's worth a try," I said.

But even adding the cobwebs and plastic spiders to the bushes didn't make it feel spookier. I'm sure the fact that the spiders were neon pink didn't help.

"Why don't you have black spiders?" I asked Wilson.

He shrugged. "The pink ones were on sale."

Le sigh.

If we couldn't get the location to work, maybe we could frame the shot to make the most of it?

I consulted with Lucy, my camerabat.

"What if we framed the shot really tightly?" I said. "So that we just see the spiderwebs?"

She made a camera frame with her fingers. "Like this?"

"Tighter," I said. "Real tight. Super-duper tight."

Lucy looked at me in exasperation.

"Any tighter and we'll need to use a microscope to film this," she said.

✩ ♡ ✩

We were using my WHIZ BANG™ to shoot the movie.

EDITING SYSTEM!

INTERNET ACCESS!

BUILT-IN CAMERA!

PHOTO STORAGE!

PHONE CALLS!

TURTLE OPERATING SYSTEM 1000.0!

VIDEOCONFERENCING!

CAN MAKE WAFFLES!

As Lucy and I started to set up the shot, Duckie walked over to me.

"We seem to be having a problem with the talent," he said.

"Which talent?"

"Felicia. She's not happy."

"What do I do?"

He shrugged. "You're the director. Make her happy."

I went over to Felicia. She was sitting in a chair and staring at her cell phone. Penny was fluffing Felicia's whiskers.

"Just about ready?" I asked her with a big smile.

She didn't look up from her screen. "Do I **look** ready?"

"You look great!"

"Well, I don't **feel** great."

"Oh," I said lamely. "You got braces."

"Yes, I got braces," she hissed. "And they hurt!"

"Can I get you something to make you feel better?"

"You can get me some croissants."

"Croissants?"

She looked up at me. "I'm supposed to be French! Also, they're soft and I'm allowed to eat them. I'm hungry."

"We have muffins on the craft service table," I said. **Craft service** is film-speak for **crew snacks.**

She snorted. "Nobody likes muffins."

"Okay," I promised her. "I'll get you some croissants."

"Make sure they're fresh," she told me. "Not the frozen kind."

BUT I'M SO LOVABLE!

"Right!" I said, trying to smile. "Fresh!"

I ran over to Duckie. "I'll be right back. I have to find some fresh croissants for Felicia."

He tapped his watch. "We're supposed to be shooting! We're burning daylight."

"I'll be back in ten minutes."

☆ ♡ ☆

Make that an hour and ten minutes. Who knew it was so hard to find fresh-baked croissants?

But croissants were just the beginning of Felicia's demands.

She wanted whisker extensions (extra thick); she wanted a new blouse (with a Peter Pan collar); and she needed throat lozenges (coconut milk). And on and on and on. Apparently, being a director had nothing to do with being in charge or having a vision. My main job was herding cats! Literally.

Finally, I managed to get Felicia to the set.

"All right," I said. "In this scene, you're being chased by Bigfoot."

"Why is he chasing me?" Felicia asked. "What's my motivation?"

"It's a dream sequence. Let's review it."

SCENE 3

EXT. SPOOKY FOREST (DREAM SEQUENCE)

VERONIQUE is sitting on a bench. BIGFOOT is peering out from behind a tree, looking menacing.

> BIGFOOT
> huff

> VERONIQUE
> What's that?

BIGFOOT lumbers behind her. VERONIQUE notices.

> VERONIQUE
>
> AAAAAAAGHHHHHHHH!

VERONIQUE starts running, with BIGFOOT chasing her. The camera follows them through the woods.

Felicia nodded. "I think I've got it."
Le sigh of relief.
"Places, folks!" Duckie shouted.
"Slate, please," I said.
Duckie stepped in with it.

"**Au Revoir, My Locker.** Scene three, take one!" he shouted, and clapped the slate.

"Action!" I shouted.

Ten takes later, I wasn't happy. The shot was kind of ... **boring.** It didn't feel nightmarish.

"This shot needs something," I muttered, looking around.

I had an idea.

A brilliant one!

"Wilson, can I borrow your skateboard?" I asked him.

"Sure," he said.

I huddled with my actors.

"Felicia, when you jump up in fright, start running. Georgie, you chase her. Lucy and I will follow you on the skateboard with the camera."

"Great idea!" Lucy said.

"I know," I replied.

We got into our places.

"**Au Revoir, My Locker.** Scene three, take eleven!" Duckie shouted.

"Action!" I shouted as Lucy aimed the WHIZ BANG™.

Then Felicia took off running with Georgie after her. I pushed the skateboard, and we started filming.

☆ ♥ ☆

At the end of the day, we had done thirty takes, but it was worth it because we had nailed the scene.

"See you tomorrow!" I told everyone.

My mom greeted me at the door when I got home.

"How was your first day of shooting, Miss Director?" she asked me.

"It was great!" I told her. "Want to see what we shot?"

"Sure," she said.

"Here, let me just hit PLAY," I told her.

"And I made you cupcakes," my mom said.

OOOOH! CUPCAKES!

"Now, the first couple of takes are a little rough," I told her. "But they start to get good around the twenty-fourth take."

"Okay," she said.

I took a bite of cupcake and waited for the video to start.

On the screen, a message flashed.

›DELETION COMPLETE‹

Cupcake crumbs flew out of my mouth. Typical.

That's <u>Amore</u>!

I was downright gloomy when I relayed the bad news to the crew the next day at lunch.

"**All the footage** was deleted?" Lucy asked.

I nodded.

They looked as shell-shocked as I felt. Nobody said anything for a moment.

Finally, Wilson sighed and patted me on the shoulder. "It's okay, Babymouse. We'll figure it out. We've got your back."

"He means we've got your whiskers," Georgie teased.

"That's pretty dangerous," Penny snorted. "Have you seen Babymouse's whiskers?"

Everyone laughed. Even me.

"Thanks, gang," I whispered.

"Let's just focus on what we're shooting tomorrow," Duckie said. For a duck, he was pretty unflappable.

Our next big scene to shoot was a love scene. As in **ooh-la-la** love! And smooches. It was supposed to take place at a café on the streets of Paris, but since there wasn't any money in the budget to fly to Paris (**très** annoying!), Duckie had suggested we shoot in the cafeteria.

Ms. Octavia even excused us from morning classes so we could shoot when the cafeteria was empty and clean.

I have to say, it was a little strange to be in the cafeteria when it was empty. The whole place still smelled like burnt pizza.

"Babymouse!" Wilson called, walking up to me with a clipboard. "I need more direction on what should be on the restaurant table. What were you thinking for tablecloths?"

To be honest, I hadn't given it any thought. I mean, who thinks about **tablecloths**?

"I don't know," I said.

He whipped out a folder and showed me pictures of tablecloth patterns. "What about checked? Crisp white? Maybe some lace?"

My head spun.

"Let's go with ... **white**," I said. That felt French-**ish**.

"What about napkins?"

"What about them?"

He rolled his eyes. "What color napkins?

Cloth or paper? Napkin holders? And what about cutlery? Do you want silverware or plastic? Maybe chopsticks?"

"Uh . . . cloth! And silverware."

I was starting to crack.

"Do you want salt and pepper shakers? Any condiments? Flowers? Candles?"

That was just the beginning.

Everyone was barraging me with questions. Penny needed more direction on costumes. Georgie needed more direction on lighting. And on and on and on.

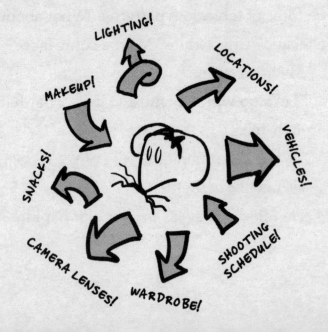

Everyone wanted direction, and I was totally . . .

It took most of the morning, but we finally got the shot set up. Henry and Felicia sat at a cafeteria table, which had been transformed into a Parisian café through Wilson's prop magic. There was a painted backdrop of Paris behind them. Even the lighting was romantic. Georgie had put pink gels on the lights, and the whole scene looked like cotton candy.

I did a quick rehearsal with the actors. Henry was playing the Mysterious Figure.

EXT. SIDEWALK CAFÉ—SUNSET

    VERONIQUE
You know I would cross an ocean for you!

    MYSTERIOUS FIGURE
I was hoping we could sail the waters together.

    VERONIQUE
Does this
mean . . . ?

```
MYSTERIOUS FIGURE
My love, will you share your life
with me?


VERONIQUE
Until my whiskers are gray!


They lean in across the table, look
into each other's eyes, and kiss.
```

"Are you both okay with everything?" I
asked them.

"You mean the kiss?" Felicia asked.

I nodded.

"Of course," she said. "We're professionals."

"I've been doing theater since first grade,"
Henry added, rolling his eyes.

"All right, then," I said. "Let's shoot!"

Duckie clapped the slate. "**Au Revoir, My
Locker.** Scene twenty-seven, take one!"

"Action!" I shouted.

☆ ♡ ☆

We had to wait until after school to do the shot again. It took us an hour to set up the scene.

Finally, our actors were in place. Time to get the film rolling!

"**Au Revoir, My Locker.** Scene twenty-seven, take two!"

"Action!" I called.

Felicia had barely delivered one line when Caden held his hand up.

"Hold on!" he shouted.

It was the first time I'd ever heard him speak, and his timing was terrible.

"What's wrong?" I demanded.

Caden looked up from his recorder. "Something's making noise. I can hear it in the background."

I looked around. The cafeteria was empty.

"It's coming from over there," Caden said, pointing at the kitchen.

I marched over to the kitchen and flung open the door.

CLEARLY, LUNCH LADIES PREFER MUSICALS.

☆ ♥ ☆

We waited until the lunch ladies left before we started shooting again.

Duckie shouted, "**Au Revoir, My Locker.** Scene twenty-seven, take three!"

"Action!" I called.

Almost immediately, Caden raised his hand.

"I hear something in the background," he said.

I whirled on him. "I don't care! I don't hear it! Stop interrupting the shoot!"

He pursed his lips. "You're the director."

"Exactly! Now ... action!"

Lucy started recording on the WHIZ BANG™.

Felicia gave Henry a smoldering glance. "You know I would cross an ocean for you!"

Henry leaned in. "I was hoping we could sail the waters together."

A gasp. "Does this mean ... ?"

"My love, will you share your life with me?"

"Until my whiskers are messy!" Felicia declared.

(She was supposed to say "Until my whiskers are gray!" But I wasn't about to stop her.)

They leaned forward, lips parted. And kissed!

It was magical! It was perfect! It was . . .

BUUUFFFFFFFFFF!!!!!

Diva Disaster

After school the next day, the whole crew met with Ms. Octavia to discuss our progress.

"So how many scenes do you have left to shoot?"

No one answered.

She looked at me. "Well, Babymouse?"

"Technically, all except one," I admitted.

She shook her head, disappointed. "You're going to have to pick up the pace.

Time is money in filmmaking. Many films are shot in under a month. No one can spend a year shooting. You need to figure out how to speed up your production."

"But how?"

"One way is to shoot multiple scenes on a single location. Part of the crew can be shooting one scene while the other part is dressing the set for the next scene. You have to keep a steady workflow."

That made sense.

"What are the locations of the scenes you want to shoot next?" she asked.

Duckie consulted his clipboard. "A bedroom, a patio on an estate in the English countryside, in front of a doorway on a Parisian street, the Amazon rain forest, and the ocean."

"Hmmm," Ms. Octavia murmured. "It sounds challenging, but I actually think it's doable. You need to break it down to basics.

Location-wise, you need a bedroom, a patio with grass in the background, a doorway, some thick exotic trees, and a body of water."

I ticked through the list in my head. "I know! We can shoot it at my house!"

"Your house, Babymouse?" Felicia scoffed. "Last time I checked, it wasn't in the English countryside."

But Ms. Octavia gave me a small smile. "Go on, Babymouse."

"All those things are at my house." And then I frowned. "Except the body of water."

"We can use a bathtub," Georgie suggested.

"I can find some miniature boats," Wilson said. "And paint a background!"

"That's a great idea!" I said. "But I still have to do one thing."

"What's that, Babymouse?" Wilson said.

I made a face. "Ask my mom."

"I don't know, Babymouse," my mother said.
"That's an awful lot of people to have in the
house."

We were in the kitchen. My annoying Little was sitting at the table doing his homework. I knew he was trying to overhear what
we were talking about. He had big ears.

"**Please**, Mom," I begged. "I can't let down
the crew. I'm the director!"

My mother narrowed her eyes. "All right.
But you have to promise two things."

"Anything!" I told her.

"One: you have to clean up after your-selves. No messes."

"Got it."

"And number two: you have to let your little brother be involved."

"Woo-hoo!" Squeak shouted.

"Why?"

She put her hands on her hips. "Because he's your little brother. Also, he lives here."

"Fine," I muttered. "He can be a PA."

"What's a PA?" Squeak asked.

"Production assistant," I told him.

"That sounds important," he said.

I grinned. "Oh, it is."

I couldn't wait to boss my Little around.

On Saturday morning, my mom and dad left to "enjoy the day," as they said.

"Make sure it's clean as a whistle when

we return," my mother called as they walked out.

"I will!" I promised.

The first scene took place on the back patio. I had some of the production assistants stand in while we set up the shot because the actors were getting their makeup put on.

"Très bien!" I declared. "Bring in the actors."

Felicia swept in, looking fabulous.

"You look wonderful, Felicia," I told her.

"Of course I do," she sniffed.

Henry walked out a minute later, looking very dapper.

"Places, everyone," I called.

"Uh, Babymouse?" Lucy whispered. "You might want to take a look at this."

"What's wrong?" I asked, walking around to look at the screen.

"Oh," I said. "Any ideas?"

"Hat?" she suggested.

"Penny, can you come over here for a moment?"

"What do you need, Babymouse?"

I pointed at the screen. "You wouldn't happen to have any top hats, would you?"

"I have a beanie," she said.

"That's not gonna work. Uh, Wilson?"

"What is taking so long?" Felicia demanded. "I'm tired of standing here!"

"Uh, just give us a minute, please," I said quickly.

"What's wrong?" Wilson asked.

I pointed at the WHIZ BANG™.

"Just stick him on an overturned box," he said.

"Good thinking!" I looked around. "Squeak! Run and get a box! And make it fast."

Squeak ran back a moment later with a box. "Here, Babymouse."

"Go tell Henry to stand on it."

A minute later, we were ready to go. **Le finally.**

Duckie clapped the slate. "**Au Revoir, My Locker.** Scene twelve, take one!"

"And . . . action!" I shouted.

THE WEATHER IS UNSEASONABLY WARM FOR YORKSHIRE.

CHANGE IS IN THE AIR.

SHOULD WE GO TO INDIA?

I HEAR THE MONSOONS— AAAGHH!

RIIIIP!

THUNK!

YOU GAVE ME A CARDBOARD BOX TO STAND ON?

AN ACTOR OF MY REPUTATION SHOULD NEVER BE GIVEN A CARDBOARD BOX!

WHAT KIND OF SET IS THIS?

HENRY!

LE SIGH.

☆ ♡ ☆

After Henry calmed down, we got the shot and moved on. We started to get into a rhythm, running the set the way Ms. Octavia had suggested.

SHOT LIST

SCENE 23: VERONIQUE HOLDING
~~A SILK PARASOL~~ *AN UMBRELLA*

CLOSE-UP
SCENE 31: ~~OVERHEAD CRANE SHOT~~
OF VERONIQUE

SCENE 33: ~~HELICOPTER SHOT OF~~
VERONIQUE ~~ON HORSEBACK IN~~
~~COUNTRYSIDE~~ *SITTING ON GRASS*

SCENE 37: VERONIQUE AND HENRY ON
~~BICYCLE BUILT FOR TWO~~ *SKATEBOARD*

SCENE 41: VERONIQUE STROLLING
AT ZOO, WITH ~~LIVE ELEPHANTS~~ *GEORGIE*
IN THE BACKGROUND

We crossed off the shot list one by one. We had to make a few changes on the fly.

I was especially worried about shooting the big ocean-crossing scene. I wanted it to look like the movie **Titanic**. Unfortunately, we didn't have a **Titanic** budget. We had a bathtub budget.

Still, it didn't look that bad: Wilson hung a backdrop of blue sky on the bathtub wall and used some of Squeak's bathtub toys in the water.

But as I reviewed it, I realized it needed one more small touch to make it seem even more authentic.

"Turn on the shower," I told Wilson. "It will look like ocean spray."

"Not a bad idea," he agreed.

It was perfect.

We got the shot in three takes—a first for the crew!

"All right!" Duckie announced. "Let's break for dinner! There's pizza in the kitchen."

As everyone headed downstairs, I remembered my mother's words about keeping the house clean.

"Squeak," I told my Little, "clean up the bathroom."

"But I'm hungry!" he whined.

"Too bad," I said with a smirk. "You're the one who wanted to be on the crew."

The last shot of the day was on the front porch. It was supposed to be in front of a doorway in Paris, and Wilson had given it some great props.

We were in the middle of the third take when Felicia's cell phone beeped.

BEEP!

She paused midshot to look down at it. Then she whispered something in Henry's ear.

The next thing I knew, they were walking off the set. I ran after them.

"Hey! Where are you going? We're in the middle of the scene!"

Felicia looked back and smirked. "Sorry, Babymouse. It's Drama Club. Their lead just got stomach flu. They need me."

Henry continued walking out with her.

"Henry? Where are you going?"

"Theater people know how to treat actors," he huffed.

Then they were gone.

I couldn't believe it. I looked at Wilson in shock. "We just lost our leads!"

"We'll figure it out," Wilson said. "Why

don't you go take a break. Grab a glass of water."

I went into the kitchen. Squeak was sitting at the table, munching on pizza.

I wanted to cry. This was a disaster! I could practically feel the tears running from my eyes, and then I realized I **wasn't** crying. Something wet was dripping on my cheeks.

I looked up and saw water pooling on the ceiling.

"Did you clean up the bathroom?" I asked.

"Yep," Squeak said.

I looked at the ceiling and then back at him.

"Did you drain the tub and turn off the shower?"

He blinked. "You didn't ask me to do that."

There's no word in French to describe the deep pit of fear in my stomach. Then again, I think **horreur** might work. (That's "horror," in case you're wondering.)

FWOOSH!?

AAAGHH!

I DON'T KNOW ABOUT EPIC, BUT THIS SURE SEEMS LIKE A DISASTER MOVIE TO ME.

UGH.

BABYMOUSE, WE'RE HOME!

Visionary

My lead actors had quit. My parents were furious at me for flooding the house. And we were way behind schedule.

My dream of being Famous had gone straight down . . . the drain.

I couldn't bear to face my crew at lunch, so I hid out in the library and surfed the Internet.

YOUR ONLINE HOROSCOPE!

GEMINI

You will *totally* fail at everything today.
Don't even bother to try.
Go back to bed.

Typical.

I headed to my favorite website. It always had the latest Hollywood gossip.

SuperFamousPeople.com

There were the usual pictures of actors, TV show hosts, and athletes. The one thing they had in common was that paparazzi were always taking embarrassing photos of them. (Did none of them have the sense to fix their whiskers before going to the grocery store?)

An article leaped out at me.

Q&A with BIG-TIME SUPERSTAR FILM DIRECTOR

The Visionary Director Talks About Fame, Fortune, and His Craft

INTERVIEWER: How do you get through a long film shoot?

I'd heard about this guy. He made some great movies about . . . uh, I forget.

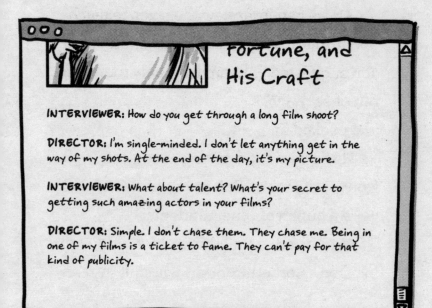

Fortune, and His Craft

INTERVIEWER: How do you get through a long film shoot?

DIRECTOR: I'm single-minded. I don't let anything get in the way of my shots. At the end of the day, it's my picture.

INTERVIEWER: What about talent? What's your secret to getting such amazing actors in your films?

DIRECTOR: Simple. I don't chase them. They chase me. Being in one of my films is a ticket to fame. They can't pay for that kind of publicity.

His words bounced around in my head. **They can't pay for that kind of publicity.** It gave me an idea.

After school, I headed to a classroom where the sign on the open door said "Student Newspaper Club."

I could hear raised voices.

"We can always do another exposé about how the lunch ladies are using cheddar instead of mozzarella on the pizza," someone said.

"Or we can interview the science teacher about the frogs that escaped," another person suggested. "I heard they only found one out of seventy."

I peeked in.

There was a girl sitting on a desk in the front of the room. Before her in a semicircle were a bunch of other students.

"We need something big!" the girl insisted. "Something that will pull in readers! The story needs to have heart!"

"Excuse me," I said with what I hoped was a winning smile. "I think I have an idea for your story."

☆ ♡ ☆

Everybody—and I mean **everybody**—was talking about me.

I was the front-page story in the student newspaper.

The School Bulletin

SPECIAL FEATURE

Visionary Director Babymouse Chats About Crafting a Winning Film

Babymouse, movie director

Babymouse gave us an exclusive interview about her upcoming film. She told us the winning formula.

"The most important ingredient is talent. And we have talented actors—Felicia and Henry."

staying true to your vision is the most important thing," said Babymouse.

Her crew works together like a finely oiled machine. All of them—camera operator, sound technician, props, wardrobe, even production assistants—are

MEATLOAF AGAIN?
Cafeteria rocked by scandal

People called my name as I walked down the hallway.

"Babymouse! Hi, Babymouse! Oooh, Babymouse!"

I was suddenly popular. And, dare I say . . . **Famous!**

Duckie was waiting for me by my locker. He was holding a copy of the student newspaper, and he didn't look happy.

"Babymouse," Duckie said. "How could you say this?"

"Say what?"

He began reading. **"Babymouse gave us an exclusive interview about her upcoming film. She told us the winning formula. 'The most important ingredient is talent. And we have talented actors—Felicia and Henry.'"** He held out his hands. "They quit, Babymouse! You lied."

"I exaggerated," I clarified. "Look, it's all part of my plan."

He looked annoyed. "What plan?"

I nodded at Felicia, who was walking toward us with Henry at her side.

"This plan."

"Babymouse," she said.

I looked at her as if surprised. "Hi, Felicia! How's theater going?"

"Well," she said casually, "the thing is, Henry and I have discovered some room in our schedules, so we can continue film-ing."

"Really? What great news! Are you sure?"

"We're sure," Henry said.

"Wonderful! We'll see you after school!" I said as they walked away.

I turned and faced Duckie.

"You got them back," he whispered, sounding impressed.

I smiled smugly. "Of course I did. I **am** a visionary, after all."

We were back on track and ready to shoot!

Duckie and I sketched out a plan of action. Our next big scene was a crowd shot, and we needed a lot of extras.

"How are we going to find all these extras?" I asked.

"Flyers around school?" Duckie suggested.

"That didn't work so well last time," I pointed out. "What if I send an email blast?"

He nodded. "Couldn't hurt."

I worked on the email blast after school.

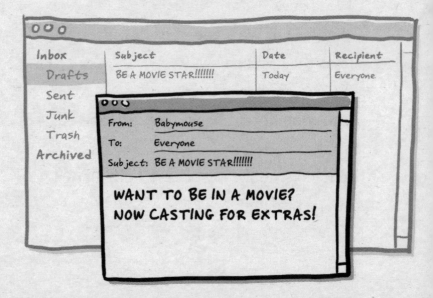

☆ ♡ ☆

The next day after school, the hallway was crowded with kids, and I had to fight my way to Film Club.

"What's with all the people?" I asked

Duckie. "Is there a sports game or something?"

He looked bewildered and shook his head. "They're all trying out to be extras. They've been lining up since the end of school! I've counted three hundred so far."

"Three hundred kids are trying out to be extras in my movie?" I asked.

He nodded.

I. Had. Arrived.

Now that we were back in the game, I decided I was going to be different. No more Miss Nice-Girl Director. I was going to be tough. I wasn't going to let anything get in the way of my shots.

Not even my own crew.

Because right away, they started complaining.

"Babymouse, I need more time to decorate the hallways so they look like Paris," Wilson said.

"No," I told him.

Penny walked up.

"I need more costumes to dress all the extras!" she begged.

"No," I told her.

Georgie was next.

"I need more lights to illuminate the hallway for the crowd shot," he pleaded.

"No," I told him.

Duckie walked up to me.

"No," I said.

He looked confused. "No what?"

"No to whatever you were going to ask for," I said. "Just no."

"Okay." He shrugged. "I was just going to see if you wanted a jelly doughnut. I got a box donated to craft service."

He turned and walked away.

Maybe I needed to rethink my whole "No" thing.

☆ ♥ ☆

The crowd scene we were filming was complex. In the scene, Henry was chasing after Veronique in a crowded street in Paris. The camera needed to follow him.

Lucy suggested that we rehearse the scene a few times. It was like choreographing a dance—having the extras walk up and down the street as the actors moved through the crowd, with the camera behind them.

After we'd done it three times, I was ready to go.

I grabbed the WHIZ BANG™ from Lucy.

"What's going on, Babymouse?" she asked me.

"I'm going to do the shot," I told her.

Lucy frowned. "What? Why?"

"Because I know what I want."

"But—but—just explain it to me," she said. "I can do it."

I shook my head. "I've got this."

Her wings folded in, and she stepped back.

Duckie clapped the slate. "**Au Revoir, My Locker.** Scene twenty-four, take one!"

"Action!" I shouted.

Like clockwork, Henry started moving after Felicia. I hit RECORD on the WHIZ BANG™ and began filming. Duckie shouted to the extras to move here and there. I passed smoothly through the crowd, and before I knew it, it was over.

I got the shot!

I was perfect.

I was a Visionary.

In the Can

Fresh off my success the day before, I sat down with Ms. Octavia and showed her the footage.

"That's very impressive, Babymouse," she said. "The crowd shot is exceptional."

"Thanks!" I said. "I did it myself."

She looked at me. "Yourself?"

"I operated the WHIZ BANG™," I explained.

"I see," she murmured.

☆ ♡ ☆

Our next few scenes would be night shoots. At lunch, I started to get pushback from my crew.

"What time will we start shooting?" Georgie asked.

I consulted my shot list. "If we start at eight p.m., we should be done right around five a.m. **If** we stay on schedule."

Penny looked shocked. "Five a.m.?"

"Well," I said, "we could start at seven p.m. That would give us more of a cushion. Also, a reporter from the student newspaper is going to be on set. She's going to do an article on the shoot."

"Babymouse," Lucy said, "we have a big math test coming up on Friday. I don't mind shooting after school, but all night?"

I was surprised. I'd thought for sure that out of everyone, **she** would be a night person.

"This film is way more important than some math test. You can always make it up."

"I need sleep," Caden said, sounding annoyed.

Wilson took my side. "Come on, gang. Babymouse is right. It's just one night. We can do this!"

I gave him a thankful smile.

"Fine," Caden grumbled. "But I don't have to be happy about it."

In spite of the complaining, the crew showed up on time the following night. It was freezing, and everybody was bundled in winter coats.

"Where's our trailer?" Felicia asked.

"Uh, we don't have one," I explained.

"How are we supposed to stay warm? We're actors. We should at least have heat lamps!" Henry insisted.

"Sorry," I told him.

Then I gathered the crew for a pep talk.

"We need to keep these shots moving along," I said as we huddled. "So let's work fast, okay?"

"If-you-say-so-Babymouse," said Georgie, shivering.

The scenes were supposed to take place on the streets of Paris. I really wanted there to be old-fashioned streetlamps in the shots, so we were shooting downtown on Main Street. It was quiet and a little eerie. All the businesses were closed.

"I've got the shot framed," Lucy called.

I went over and looked through the WHIZ BANG™.

"That garbage can's not working," I told Wilson.

"The garbage can?"

"It's not French enough."

He looked at me. "What does a French garbage can look like, Babymouse?"

All these little details were distracting me!

"Do I have to do everything myself?" I shouted. I marched over to the garbage can and dragged it out of the shot.

Wilson just sighed.

Then I grabbed the WHIZ BANG™ from Lucy's hands.

"I'm gonna shoot this," I told her. "It's too complicated to explain."

Her mouth thinned into a line.

"If you say so, Babymouse," she said.

"Slate, please!" I ordered.

"**Au Revoir, My Locker.** Scene thirty-three, take one!" Duckie called.

And we were rolling.

It grew colder and colder as the night went on.

By three in the morning, even I was shivering. But we still had two big shots to get in the can. Unfortunately, there wasn't enough light from the streetlamps. We had brought lights from the Film Club equipment closet. Georgie arranged them on set and huddled with Duckie.

"Almost ready over there?" I called to them.

LOCAL WEATHER

10:00 p.m.	35° F
12:00 a.m.	25° F
3:00 a.m.	15° F

"Uh, give us a minute, Babymouse," Duckie called back.

"I'm cold, Babymouse!" Felicia whined, stomping her foot.

"Let me see what's going on," I told her.

I walked over to Georgie and Duckie.

"What's the holdup?" I asked.

Georgie held out the electrical cord. "Nowhere to plug in the lights, Babymouse. If one of the stores was open, we could probably ask them. But everything's closed."

"But we need light!"

Duckie just shrugged. "Georgie's right, Babymouse."

This was ridiculous!

"I'll figure it out myself!" I snapped, and grabbed the extension cord, marching around. How hard could it be to find an electrical outlet?

I found one right away.

"Here's one!" I shouted.

"Babymouse," Georgie cautioned me. "You can't tie in to that. Don't you see the warning?"

"We're only going to plug in the lights for one shot. What's the big deal?"

"Babymouse—"

I wasn't about to let something as little as an electrical cord stand between me and Fame.

I plugged in the cord. Did the world end? No.

"See? Wasn't that easy?" I said, and walked over to the lights.

"Uh, Babymouse . . . ," said Georgie.

I flicked on the switch for the lights and—

CITY MAIN
ELECTRICAL

DO NOT
TOUCH.

DEATH!

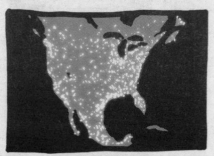

After the small "taking down the electrical grid" problem, we decided to stick with available light.

"Set up the shot again!" I shouted.

Lucy shook her head.

"I'm going home," she announced. "I'm tired. There's no reason for me to be here if I'm not even allowed to operate the WHIZ BANG™."

Nobody said anything as she flew off set.

The reporter from the newspaper came over to me.

"Is it normal to have these sorts of disagreements on set?" she asked me.

I reddened. "Of course! This is a creative field."

She scribbled something down on her pad.

"Excuse me," I said, walking over to the crew. "Come on! Move faster! We need to get these shots in the can!"

Penny stepped forward.

"You're being too bossy, Babymouse."

"I **am** the boss. I'm the director! This is **my** film!"

She shook her head. "That's where you're wrong."

Without another word, she walked off set.

A moment later, Felicia and Henry strode by me.

"Wait! Where are **you** going?" I asked them.

"This film is a joke," Felicia said. "You couldn't direct your way out of a paper bag."

"I can't believe we've been standing around without heat lamps," Henry added. "Nobody gives actors any respect!"

Next was Georgie. I shook my head in disbelief as he walked by.

Georgie shrugged. "Sorry, Babymouse," he murmured, and was followed by Caden and Duckie.

Then it was just me and Wilson.

He looked at me. Surely, my best friend wouldn't . . .

But he just gave me a disappointed look.

And walked away.

Queen of the Castle

My crew had quit. It was like being reverse-fired. Or something.

I was too embarrassed to even go into the cafeteria at lunch. I hid out in the girls' bathroom.

But that was just the beginning.

A few days later, I heard people saying my name as I went down the hallway.

Then I saw it.

The School Bulletin

EGOTISTICAL DIRECTOR ON RAMPAGE!

CREW WALKS OFF SET!

ACTRESS CONFESSES: "She's a total hack."

Everyone knows that movies are all about drama—but some... the times... pulls off the

just look at those whiskers," said Furrypaws. "You can tell she doesn't know what she's doing."

Babymouse, notorious tyrant

CHECKMATE
Is Chess Club the place to find true love?

I couldn't believe it!

I DON'T KNOW ABOUT FAMOUS, BUT PEOPLE ARE CERTAINLY PAYING ATTENTION TO YOU, BABYMOUSE.

UGH.

☆ ♡ ☆

After school, I went home and shut myself in my bedroom. I'd never felt lonelier in my entire life.

Someone knocked at the door.

"Come in," I said, not getting up from bed.

It was Squeak.

"Can I borrow your WHIZ BANG™ charger? My battery's dead."

"Okay. You can take the WHIZ BANG™, too," I told him in a dull voice. "I don't care."

"Really?" he asked. "I thought you were using it to make your movie."

"Not anymore," I muttered, and rolled on my side away from him. "Everybody's mad at me. My crew quit."

"What'd you do to make them quit?"

"What did **I** do?"

That was when I realized. Sure, middle school might be a monster movie.

But **I** was the one who was the monster.

"I didn't even stop to think about what my crew wanted," I whispered. "Or how I was treating them. I was a terrible director."

He looked at me.

"Why don't you just say you're sorry, Babymouse?"

"Say I'm sorry?"

"Yeah. It's pretty easy, Babymouse," he said.

Could he be right? Was it really that easy?

Squeak walked to the door, shaking his head. "Seriously. Middle schoolers have no brains."

☆ ♡ ☆

My crew was sitting at our usual table when I walked up, carrying a box of cupcakes. They didn't look happy to see me. Wilson wouldn't even meet my eyes; he just stared at his tray. It stung. Maybe this was a dumb idea after all. But I had to try.

"Uh, guys," I said, swallowing nervously. "I'm sorry."

Nobody said anything, so I started talking. And once I started, I couldn't stop. The words just poured out of me.

"I didn't mean to turn into a monster director. I got so focused on the film and what it would do for me that I forgot it was your film, too. I let my ego take over, and I didn't stop to think about you guys. I thought I could do it by myself, and I was completely wrong. I know I'm the worst director ever, and if you never forgive me, I would understand, and I'm so, so sorry and I feel terrible and—"

Wilson interrupted me. "Cut!"

I looked at him in surprise.

Lucy rolled her eyes. "We get it, Babymouse."

"And we forgive you," Penny said.

Relief flooded me right down to my whiskers.

"Thanks," I whispered.

"What's in the box?" Georgie asked.

I opened the lid.

Lucy laughed. "Now, **that's** a sweet
apology."

☆ ♡ ☆

With my crew's faith in me restored, I felt like I was Queen of the World!

Which was good because I had a medieval-size problem to solve for our last day of shooting.

I needed to find a castle. And, surprisingly, there weren't a lot of castles in town.

Duckie and I jumped on the public bus to check out possible locations.

The first few were underwhelming.

Our last stop was "Ye Olde Castle Times."
It was a medieval fair.

I gasped in delight.

It was perfect!

It was castle-rific!

"Look! There's even a turret! It will be so romantic."

"Babymouse," Duckie said.

"Maybe we can shoot when the sun is setting."

"Uh, Babymouse," Duckie said, and pointed.

My whiskers fell.

"But . . . this is the perfect location!" I cried.

"Well," Duckie said, rubbing his chin, "I guess we can shoot it guerrilla-style."

"What's that?"

"We just sneak in and shoot," Duckie explained. "Don't ask for permission. We won't be able to rehearse or set up lights or anything. We'll just wing it."

"I'm good with that!" I said.

He grinned at me. "All right, then. Let's get this film in the can."

☆ ♥ ☆

The day of the castle shoot, we met in my garage to get the actors dressed and in makeup.

I was in my bedroom making last-minute script changes. I needed to shorten the scenes because Duckie was worried that if we lingered too long in one spot, we would be kicked out.

SCENE 54

EXT. CASTLE (ENGLISH COUNTRYSIDE)

The sun is setting as the camera pushes in
TIGHT on VERONIQUE'S FACE and THE
MYSTERIOUS FIGURE.

> VERONIQUE
> ~~How did we ever get to this place? I~~
> ~~hoped and dreamed that you would~~
> ~~come to me, but after all this time~~
> ~~and all the turmoil, what can we do?~~
> ~~The dukedom is lost to my family~~
> ~~forever. No one will ever recognize~~
> ~~the Locker crest on my family's flag~~
> ~~as it waves above the turret of the~~
> ~~castle. And I cannot but wish we~~
> ~~could go back in time to our younger~~
> ~~days, when we both cavorted on this~~
> ~~lawn with the sun shining down and~~
> ~~when everything seemed so possible.~~

Wassup?

There was a knock at the door.

"Come in!" I called.

"Babymouse, we're having a problem

with the talent," Penny said. "Felicia and Henry both called in sick."

"Both of them?"

She shrugged. "There's a nasty stomach flu going around."

"So what're we going to do?"

"Don't worry," Penny assured me. "I have it all figured out. Follow me."

When we got to the garage, she pointed. "What do you think?"

Le super-duper grand sigh.

Penny made a face. "Sorry, Babymouse. I did the best I could."

"No! It's fine! They look great!" I quickly assured her. "We can shoot them from behind anyway."

Duckie clapped. "Come on, crew! Daylight's burning! Let's hit it!"

We piled into my mom's minivan, and she drove us to the medieval fair. The whole crew had dressed for the occasion.

Before we started to shoot our first scene, I walked over to Lucy and handed her the WHIZ BANG™.

"I was hoping you'd shoot today," I told her.

"I can do that, Babymouse," she said with a small smile.

We operated like a well-run machine, and the best part was that nobody paid attention to us. We fit right in.

The sun was setting as we prepared for the last shot of the day. I wanted to capture the magic hour—the time just before sunset, when everything is golden.

Moving quickly, we got our actors into place.

"Action!" I loud-whispered.

Georgie and Wilson leaned toward each other in silhouette, the sun slowly sliding down, bathing the whole shot in a beautiful light.

And then something small and round flew through the frame.

"What was that?" I demanded.

Another one whizzed by.

I stared at the screen.

"What's going on? Is that a UFO?" I asked Lucy.

She shook her head and pointed. "No, it's a clown."

BONK!

OUCH! MY WHISKER!

STUPID CLOWNS.

RUB RUB

TECHNICALLY, BABYMOUSE, THEY'RE JESTERS.

Final Cut

In spite of all the **clown-terference,** we got our shot. The picture was in the can.

In film-speak, it was a wrap.

Still, we weren't finished yet. Even though we had shot all the scenes, they weren't in any kind of order. Now I had to edit the raw footage into a movie.

But I was ready to go!

Besides, how hard could it be?

FILM-EDITING
DEGREE OF DIFFICULTY

☐   Easy-Peasy Lemon-Squeezy

☐   Piece of Cake

☑   Manned Mission to Mars

There was an editing software program on the computer in the Film Club room. I fired up the computer and got to work.

Editing a film was harder than keeping straight whiskers.

☆ ♥ ☆

I was trying to open stupid Locker when Georgie dipped his head down.

"Need some help, Babymouse?" he asked.

"In more ways than one," I admitted.

"What's wrong?"

"I can't figure out the editing software! I haven't even figured out how to download the footage. At this rate, the film will never be finished."

He tilted his head. "I'm pretty good at that sort of stuff, Babymouse. Why don't I give it a whirl?"

"Really? That would be so great!"

"No problem," he said. Then he banged on my locker, and it popped open.

"Thanks," I said.

We sat down in front of the monitors. Georgie had the keyboard in front of him.

"We shot a lot of video," he said.

"We did?" I asked.

He peered at the monitor. "Looks like we've got close to fourteen hours' worth."

"How long is the movie supposed to be?"

"Ninety minutes, tops," he said.

I groaned. "We're going to be here forever."

"Pretty much," he agreed.

We spent hours in the editing room selecting our favorite takes of scenes. Then we started cutting it together. It was slow going but worth it because when we were done, we had a rough cut of the film.

The only problem was that it was long.

Really long.

Five and a half hours long, to be exact.

"We need to cut some scenes," Georgie said.

So we started to trim our film down. It was painful. Every time I had to take a scene out, a little part of me died.

After working late into the night for days on end, we had a new rough cut.

"How long is it now?"

"Four hours and fifty-four minutes," Georgie replied.

Le sigh.

I had no choice. I had to be ruthless when it came to cutting scenes.

But just as soon as we solved one problem, another appeared.

It turned out that a lot of the audio from

our footage was bad. As in, you-couldn't-hear-a-word-the-actors-said bad. And, unfortunately, most of the bad audio was from Felicia.

And she'd quit. Typical.

"Maybe you can have someone else record her lines and dub them in," Wilson suggested as we waited in the lunch line one day.

I'd thought of that, too. "I don't think it will work because we'd have to have that person re-record **all** of Felicia's lines in the film. That would take forever."

I was still trying to come up with a solution when I walked into the editing room after school.

"Babymouse," Georgie said. "We have company."

Felicia was sitting right next to Georgie.

"**Bonjour,** Babymouse!" she said.

"Uh, hi," I said.

"So I understand you need me to re-record some lines," she said.

"Yes! We do! We can record you right now."

"Not so fast, Babymouse," she said. "What's in it for me?"

I didn't know what to say. "What do you want?"

A crafty look came over her face.

"I was thinking in return for re-recording my lines, I would get a producer credit."

"But you didn't do any producing!" I exclaimed. "Duckie did everything."

"Your call, Babymouse," she said, moving as if to climb out of her chair. Georgie's eyes met mine.

"Fine," I said. "You can have a producer credit."

"On second thought," she said with a

smarmy smile, "better make it **executive producer**."

☆ ♥ ☆

Duckie wasn't very happy when he learned about Felicia, but I had other things to worry about.

Musical things.

I had given Georgie a playlist of songs from the Internet to use in the movie, and he'd informed me that we couldn't use them.

"But why not?" I asked him.

"Can you afford to pay a royalty to the musicians who made the music?"

"I can't pay anything," I said, shaking my head.

"You have to get someone to make you original music," he told me.

That night at dinner, I felt overwhelmed.

"What's wrong, Babymouse?" my mother asked me.

I explained the whole music situation to her.

"Hmmm," she said. "You know, your grandfather's very musical. And he plays piano. Maybe you should talk to him."

Well, beggars couldn't be choosers.

I called Grampamouse on the phone.

"What kind of music are you looking for?" Grampa asked me.

"I need a few different pieces," I explained. "Some romantic music for the love scenes, some sweeping music for the introduction, and something moody for the mysterious parts. Ooh! And something fast-tempo and galloping for the horse-riding scenes!"

"No problem," he said. "Why don't you come over tomorrow and you can record me."

The next day, my grandfather met me at the door when I arrived.

With his . . . accordion?

"But I thought you'd be playing the piano," I said.

"The piano's out of tune, and the tuner can't come until next week. Besides, everyone likes the accordion. It's classic!"

As he started playing, I realized he was right. The accordion was classic.

Classically awful.

We had one last thing we needed to take care of, and that was the poster for the movie.

I decided to design it myself on the computer. I stayed up all night working on it and was really happy with the result.

But when I showed it to the crew after school, everyone had an opinion. And I mean everyone.

Au Revoir,
My Locker

A FILM BY BABYMOUSE

STARRING FELICIA FURRYPAWS • HENRY HIGGINS • GEORGIE GIRAFFE
DIRECTOR OF PHOTOGRAPHY LUCY FUGUS • SOUND RECORDING CADEN KODIAK
EXECUTIVE PRODUCER FELICIA FURRYPAWS • PRODUCER DUCKIE MALLARD
COSTUME DESIGN, WARDROBE, MAKEUP PENNY POODLE • SET DRESSING & PROPS WILSON WEASEL
LIGHTING GEORGIE GIRAFFE • PRODUCTION ASSISTANT SQUEAK

"You should put the Eiffel Tower on the poster," Wilson said. "That's the best scene in the movie."

"You should put Bigfoot on it," Georgie said.

"You should put ME on it," Felicia said.

Even Squeak put in his two cents.

"You should definitely put the boat shot on it," he said.

In the end, I put everything on it.

Red Carpet

inally, we had a finished film!

"We're done!" I told Ms. Octavia at our next Film Club meeting.

"Brilliant!" she told us. "We'll have a screening at school two weeks from today."

We jumped up and down in happiness.

"You should plan to dress nicely for the screening. The whole crew will come up onstage afterward to talk about the process of making the film."

If I was going to be seen by the entire middle school, I needed to look good. I needed to look great.

I needed to look . . .

BABYMOUSETASTIC!

BABYMOUSETASTIC!

BABYMOUSETASTIC!

BABYMOUSETASTIC!

BABYMOUSETASTIC!

I ran through the contents of my wardrobe in my head. My everyday look of leggings and a T-shirt was not going to work for the screening. They did not shout "Red carpet." In fact, I had no idea what they shouted. Maybe "Cafeteria"?

It was clear this was going to require a trip to the mall.

I raced home after school to tell my mom.

"Our film is going to be screened in front of the whole middle school! Can we go shopping?"

"Babymouse," she said, "do you have money saved in your allowance to buy a new dress?"

I looked at the whiteboard on the kitchen wall.

BABYMOUSE	SQUEAK
$85	$15
+ $15 babysitting	+ $50 birthday money from Grampamouse
− $500 flooded bathroom	
TOTAL:	
(− $400)	$65

Ugh! What was I going to do?

MAYBE YOU CAN BORROW SOME MONEY FROM SQUEAK, BABYMOUSE.

BUT HOW AM I GOING TO PAY FOR MY WHISKER UPDO?

☆ ♡ ☆

In the end, my mom took me shopping. (I had to promise I would babysit Squeak for free for the next year.)

Le annoying sigh.

I wanted to find the perfect dress. Something that shouted that I looked "directorial."

The day of the screening, the film crew met at the theater. Everyone was in their best duds.

"Time to go in!" Ms. Octavia announced.

All the students were already seated when we walked down the red carpet on the center aisle. (Technically, it was more of a brown carpet that might have been red at some point. It was hard to say.)

Suddenly, it felt real.

"Excuse me!" a kid called from the crowd. "I'm from the student TV station. Can you spell your name for me?"

"Of course," I told him. "It's Babymouse. B-A-B-Y-M-O-U-S-E. One word. Like Madonna."

"Not you," he said, shaking his head at me. "I meant **her**."

He pointed past my shoulder.

I turned around and almost choked. Holding court on the red (brown) carpet was . . .

Le I-give-up sigh.

☆ ♡ ☆

I settled into my seat in the same row as the rest of the crew. Wilson sat next to me.

"Are you nervous, Babymouse?"

I nodded.

He patted my hand. "It's gonna be great!"

Then the lights went dark. The title of our movie came up, and my heart started pounding fast.

DIRECTED BY
Babymouse

Then I was swept away by the action on the screen.

☆ ♡ ☆

When the film ended, the theater was completely silent.

Clearly, everyone had been deeply touched by the film. I could already see the headlines for the reviews:

The School Bulletin

Au Revoir, My Locker Is an Epic Masterpiece by a Directorial Genius!

And then it started. Not applause, but . . .

. . . **laughter?**

"That was the funniest thing I've ever seen!" I heard a kid hoot behind me.

"Hilarious!" another chortled.

"Loved the clowns!" said a third.

The laughter just kept coming. Not a single kid in the auditorium could stop cracking up.

I looked at my crew. They looked at me. I looked at them some more. They looked at me again. (It was like a bad montage sequence.)

That was when I knew I'd gotten it all wrong. Middle school wasn't a monster movie.

It was a comedy.

A **bad** comedy.

Onstage, Ms. Octavia said, "Now for a few words from the members of the crew. First, we have the director, Babymouse."

Glossary of Important Film Terms

ACTION! What the director says to tell the actors to start performing a scene.

BACKDROP: Painting of a background scene.

CAST: The actors.

CLOSE-UP: A tightly framed camera shot.

CRAFT SERVICE: Snacks on set for the crew and actors.

CREW: The people who do all the behind-the-scenes work (basically, everyone besides the actors).

CUT! What the director says to stop filming.

EDITING: Putting filmed scenes together, cutting them where needed, so they form a complete movie.

EPIC: An expensive costumed film with historical scope.

EXTRA: A minor cast member who has a nonspeaking role (such as someone in a crowd).

IN THE CAN: When a shot is finished. In the old days, film actually was stored in a metal canister.

LOCATION: A real place (not a set) where a scene is filmed.

MAGIC HOUR: Right before the sun sets, when the sky may be golden pink.

PA: Production assistant, who helps everyone else on the crew.

PRODUCER: The person who manages the production of a film. May also be a financier.

PROP: An object used in a scene (short for "property").

SLATE: A board that shows the scene number, with a stick on top—the clapper—that is snapped down to mark the beginning of a new take.

THAT'S A WRAP! Announcement at the end of shooting.

WATCH OUT, MIDDLE SCHOOL!
Babymouse has a smartphone, and she's not afraid to use it!

Turn the page for a peek at the next book!

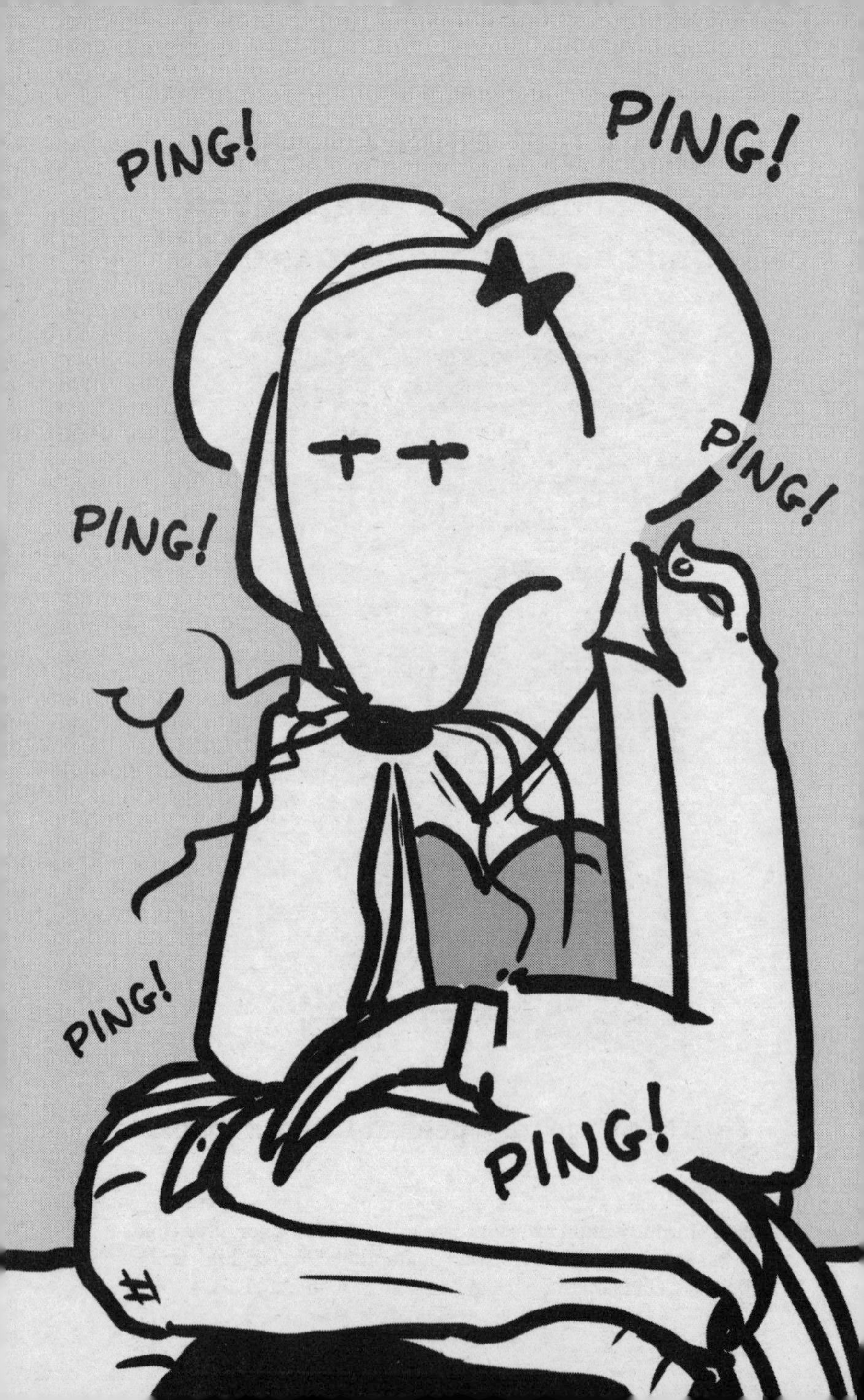
PING!
PING!
PING!
PING!
PING!
PING!

Conversation

So there I was, sitting on the bus on the way to school. And not just any school...

MIDDLE SCHOOL.

Dun. Dun. Dun.

I wanted to catch up with my friends, but everywhere I looked, kids were zoned out on their phones....

What was I supposed to do? Twiddle my thumbs?

Le sigh.

Felicia Furrypaws and her crew were sitting in front of me, texting each other. They were laughing hysterically. Why they were texting when they were sitting right next to each other, I couldn't tell you. . . .

I leaned over the back of their seat.

"What's so funny?" I asked.

All four girls stopped texting and looked up from their phones.

"Nothing, Babymouse," Felicia replied coolly.

"None of your business," Melinda added.

"Wouldn't you like to know?" Belinda asked.

"She totally would," Berry answered.

The air filled with laughter—I mean, LOLs.

Hmmph. I slumped back into my seat and wondered what they could be texting about.

Everyone stopped and looked up at me—even the bus driver, who had just pulled up to the school. I could hear crickets chirping outside.

Felicia rolled her eyes. "You are so weird sometimes, Babymouse."

I thought things might get better once I got inside the building, but I was wrong. Kids were walking up and down the hallways texting, not even bothering to look where they were going—which, as it turned out, was almost always directly into ME.

RINGGGG.

I squeaked into homeroom just in time. Mr. Ludwig, my lizard homeroom teacher, didn't even look up from his device. I turned toward my best friend, Wilson. At least **he** would pay attention to me.

"Hey, Wilson," I whispered. "How was your weekend?"

"One sec, Babymouse," he said, putting up a finger. "I just got to the good part!"

Sigh. **Let me know what that feels like,** I thought.

The first class of the day was social studies. I took my seat and pulled out my notebook and a pen.

"Now remember, class," Mr. Gibbons said. "Your reports on ancient Rome are due in a few weeks. As the saying goes, Rome wasn't built in a day, and I hope none of your projects will be, either." He walked up and down the aisles as he spoke.

"I'm sure I don't have to remind you that this assignment makes up eighty percent of your grade, so please do not wait until the last minute."

Mr. Gibbons looked directly at me, though I had no idea why. Okay, maybe I had a **little** hint. Last time we had a huge assignment like this—our ancient Egypt report—I waited until the night before to get started. Well, needless to say, that ended up being a pretty terrible idea, because I had to pull an all-nighter to get it done in time.

Still, I'm not sure how Mr. Gibbons would
have known that. . . .

I was mostly tuning my teacher out, because it just so happened that I had finished my project early. I really didn't want history to repeat itself (and neither did my parents).

☆ ♥ ☆

The rest of the day fell as flat as Felicia's pin-straight whiskers. I couldn't strike up a conversation with any of my friends. It seemed like all anyone cared about was updating their statuses, posting selfies, or checking in to different classrooms. With all the checking in, you'd think the school was a hotel.

☆ ♥ ☆

When I got home, I plopped in front of the TV like a character from one of Wilson's zombie movies. TV made everything better. Usually. But instead, I was taunted by commercial after commercial—every single ad was for the Whiz Bang™ phone!

HAVE YOU READ ALL THE BOOKS IN THE SERIES?

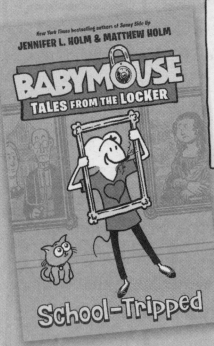

Will a class field trip with **no chaperones** be as thrilling as Babymouse thinks? Or will life in the Big City trip her up big-time?

New York Times bestselling authors of Sunny Side Up

JENNIFER L. HOLM & MATTHEW HOLM

BABYMOUSE
TALES FROM THE LOCKER

Whisker Wizard

Babymouse is a
whisker influencer!
But can her internet
fame last forever?

Will Babymouse's performance
be a showstopper . . .
or should someone actually
try to stop her?